Not human,
not wolf, neither and
both.

Books By
C.M. STUNICH

Romance Novels

HARD ROCK ROOTS SERIES
Real Ugly
Get Bent
Tough Luck
Bad Day
Born Wrong
Hard Rock Roots Box Set (1-5)
Dead Serious
Doll Face
Heart Broke
Get Hitched
Screw Up

TASTING NEVER SERIES
Tasting Never
Finding Never
Keeping Never
Tasting, Finding, Keeping: The Story of Never Box Set (1-3)
Never Can Tell
Never Let Go
Never Did Say
Never Have I

ROCK-HARD BEAUTIFUL
Groupie
Roadie
Moxie

THE BAD NANNY TRILOGY
Bad Nanny
Good Boyfriend
Great Husband

TRIPLE M SERIES
Losing Me, Finding You
Loving Me, Trusting You
Needing Me, Wanting You

Craving Me, Desiring You

A DUET
Paint Me Beautiful
Color Me Pretty

FIVE FORGOTTEN SOULS
Beautiful Survivors
Alluring Outcasts

MAFIA QUEEN
Lure
Lavish
Luxe

DEATH BY DAYBREAK MC
I Was Born Ruined

STAND-ALONE NOVELS
Baby Girl
All for 1
Blizzards and Bastards (originally featured in the Snow and Seduction Anthology)
Fuck Valentine's Day (A Short Story)
Broken Pasts
Crushing Summer
Taboo Unchained
Taming Her Boss
Kicked

Violet Blaze Novels
(MY PEN NAME)

BAD BOYS MC TRILOGY
Raw and Dirty
Risky and Wild
Savage and Racy

Books By
C.M. STUNICH

HERS TO KEEP TRILOGY
Biker Rockstar Billionaire CEO Alpha
Biker Rockstar Billionaire CEO Dom
Biker Rockstar Billionaire CEO Boss

STAND-ALONE
Football Dick
Stepbrother Thief
Stepbrother Inked
Glacier

Fantasy Novels

THE SEVEN MATES OF ZARA WOLF
Pack Ebon Red
Pack Violet Shadow
Pack Obsidian Gold
Pack Ivory Emerald
Pack Amber Ash
Pack Azure Frost
Pack Crimson Dusk

SIRENS OF A SINFUL SEA TRILOGY
Under the Wild Waves

THE SEVEN WICKED SERIES
Seven Wicked Creatures
Six Wicked Beasts
Five Wicked Monsters
Four Wicked Fiends

HOWLING HOLIDAYS SHORT STORIES
A Werewolf Christmas
A Werewolf New Year's
A Werewolf Valentine's
A Werewolf St. Patrick's Day

A Werewolf Spring Break
A Werewolf Mother's Day

ACADEMY OF SPIRITS AND SHADOWS
Spirited

OTHER FANTASY NOVELS
Gray and Graves
Indigo & Iris
She Lies Twisted
Hell Inc.
DeadBorn
Chryer's Crest

Co-Written
(With Tate James)

HIJINKS HAREM
Elements of Mischief
Elements of Ruin
Elements of Desire

THE WILD HUNT MOTORCYCLE CLUB
Dark Glitter

FOXFIRE BURNING
The Nine

THE SEVEN MATES 2 OF ZARA WOLF

C.M. STUNICH

INTERNATIONAL BESTSELLING AUTHOR

Pack Violet Shadow
Copyright © C.M. Stunich 2017

ISBN-10: 1981600094 (pbk.)
ISBN-13: 978-1-981600090(pbk.)
www.cmstunich.com

Cover art by Amanda Carroll
"Caviar Dreams" Font © Lauren Oliver
"Fancy Card Text" Font © Deiter Steffmann

this book is dedicated to my readers for their unfailing patience, support, and love.

you never cease to amaze me.

Character List

The Seven Mates of Zara Castille, Heir of Pack Ebon Red
First Name, Last Name, and Pack Affiliation
(in order of appearance)

Nic Hallett of Pack Ebon Red

~

Jaxson Kidd of Pack Azure Frost

~

Silas Vetter of Pack Obsidian Gold

~

Anubis Rothburg of Pack Crimson Dusk

~

Montgomery Graves of Pack Ivory Emerald

~

Che Nocturne of Pack Violet Shadow

~

Tidus Hahn of Pack Amber Ash

I threw the severed head at my mother's feet, spattering blood across her pale toes.

I was panting, shaking, my hands curled into fists by my sides. According to the rules of the Hunt, I should be dressed up in my finest, presenting my kill to the reigning Alpha Female with grace and dignity. Instead, I was naked and dirty and pissed off.

My mates stood behind me in a triangular formation, their mixed emotions perfuming the air with anger, excitement, even lust. There was so much—too much, really—going on for me to pinpoint who was feeling what. Of course, I didn't need a seer's divination to tell me that Nic Hallett was furious. He was doing a decent job of holding back, but my mother would sense it anyway; she always did.

"What's this?" Nikolina asked, leaning forward, her bloodred hair sliding over her shoulders, droplets of copper liquid draining down her chest and over her bare breasts, teased from her skin by the silver necklace that draped over her graceful neck.

"Zara of Ebon Red," I managed to choke out, falling

back on tradition to buy myself some time. I was still reeling from what I'd seen in the forest—and I had no idea how I was going to present that information to the packs. If I told my mother the truth, she'd take action in a big and violent way, a show of bravado and strength that we couldn't afford. At the same time, I had to tell her *something.*

Nikolina sat there staring at me from eyes the color of a night sky, one devoid of moon and stars. It was open and limitless, full of possibilities but impossible to understand. That was my mother, the current Alpha Female of Pack Ebon Red, in a nutshell.

She glanced down at the head of the bull moose at her feet, examining the velvety rack of antlers, the sightless eyes, the smattering of red blood where my teeth had severed the creature's neck from its body. It felt like an empty kill. Not only had I been too stressed to actually eat any of it—and in too much of a hurry to get back here to bring the unused meat with me—but I'd also been too busy having sex to actually make the killing blow with my own jaws.

"Zara Wolf," she said finally, lounging back in a throne made entirely of antlers. It was sitting outside, legs buried in the snow and flanked by torches made of animal fat. The air stunk of it, of meat and burning things. The fact that tiny flakes of snow were falling, settling on our bare skin, didn't disturb a single one of us. Werewolves were nearly impervious to cold. "What is the meaning of this?"

"We …" I started to speak when I noticed Nikolina's nostrils flaring. She was scenting me, pulling in more information than I could possibly provide with words alone. If only I had a little more of that witch hazel spray Anubis had used on me and Nic before … Somehow, I was going to have to make friends with a witch. Hilarious thought that, considering their leader had fed me the flesh of my own pack mate last time I'd been in their presence.

"You've mated with the Alpha Son of Pack Violet Shadow," she said loudly, clearly intending her words to carry across the clearing. Spread out across the snow covered ground behind me and my mates were tables heaped with food—partridges stuffed with apricots, pan-seared venison with rosemary and dried cherries, skewered sweetbreads, and black pudding potato cakes topped with fried eggs—as well as the wolves feasting from them. They lounged on chaises and chairs, under trees blanketed in fresh powdery snow, and on their sides with tongues lolling, hot breath frosting in the cool air.

At the news of my mating, howls and yips and human shouts pierced the quiet calm of the gathering.

I ignored it all. Yes, it *was* kind of a big deal that Che Nocturne and I had had sex. And it was also sort of a big deal how it happened, how angry Nic was, how mixed my own emotions were.

It was an even bigger deal that we'd seen a vampire walking in the sun.

Oh, and met a faerie queen.

"You reek of fae," Nikolina whispered, sliding off of her throne and moving close to me. I let her put her nose to my hair, drag in a long, deep breath. When she pressed a kiss to my forehead, the act was menacing at best. "Why?"

"We had a visit from the Unseelie Queen," I said as slowly and calmly as I was able. Each syllable that managed to scrape past my lips left a tiny cloud of white in the air. "She has information she wants to trade."

I kept my gaze away from the Alpha Female of Pack Ebon Red and hoped that she'd take my lack of eye contact as respectful deference instead of what it really was—a poor attempt to cover up a half-lie. We *had* entertained a visit from the faerie queen while in the forest, but it was so much more than that. We hadn't been offered a simple debriefing —we'd been offered help. Help against the vampires from Kingdom Ironbound and the witches from Coven Triad.

"Why would a faerie have information about our missing pack members?" Nikolina said, her mouth pressed so tight to my ear that even my grandmother, now standing just a few feet behind her, would have a difficult time hearing the question.

"I don't know," I said, and the words came out harsher, sharper than I'd intended.

My mother froze, every muscle in her body going stiff. For a moment there, I was sure she was going to throw me to the icy ground, pin me by the throat, and show every 'were' in attendance that even though I was her heir, she was still the fucking boss.

"Get out of here and go clean up," she said instead, stepping back with a wicked sharp smile etched onto her face. "The Alpha-Daughter of Ebon Red brings us news of our missing family members," she announced as she turned toward my grandmother, ignoring the shifting and murmuring emanating from the group. Nikolina Castille was Alpha of Pack Ebon Red; she could give as much or as little information as she wanted to the pack. No matter how desperate they were to know more, nobody other than another alpha would dare ask.

I knew what a suggestion sounded like ... and when an order was being issued.

That was most definitely an order.

"Let's go," I told the boys, turning toward the Pairing House.

I didn't look at anyone as I crunched through the snow in my bare feet, not even when they started cheering and howling in excitement. If the packs knew what sort of news I'd been privy to, the last thing they'd be doing was celebrating.

No, if they found out what the boys and I knew ... violence would be the only item on the menu.

"Do you mind if I take the first shower, *Alpha?*" Nic snapped as soon as we were inside the front door, moving past me and heading for the downstairs bathroom without waiting for an answer. He was too mad to care about protocol and rules right now.

"Nic," I said as he stormed past me and around the

staircase, letting himself into the study and then slamming the bathroom door behind him. I was too tired, too stressed to follow after him. Instead, I flopped down on the couch and found Che Nocturne sliding onto the cushions next to me.

"He'll get over it," he said in that rich, velvety voice of his. If I were a witch, and I wanted to mimic the Alpha-Son of Pack Violet Shadow's voice, I would mix grumbles, growls, chocolate, and leather into my potion. That rough but sensual voice of his was juxtaposed against his scent—vanilla, lavender and bergamot oil. He smelled sweet, sounded sinful, and burned like fire when he touched me. No wonder I'd had trouble resisting during the Hunt. Not only had the primal act of hunting in a pack stirred the bestial side of my nature, the man was just fucking attractive in his own right.

"You don't know Nic Hallett like I do," I said with a small, tired laugh. I ran a palm down my face and it came away smeared with blood. The coppery scent competed with Che's smell for control of my nostrils. When I glanced over at him, I saw that his pale skin was clean. Right. Because he hadn't killed the moose—he'd been too busy fucking me in the woodsy debris—and he hadn't severed the head like I had.

Che and I stared at each other, my eyes charcoal black and his, the blue-red color of violets.

We mated.

We *mated*.

In the woods.

Like animals.

I sucked in a deep breath and stood up, suddenly aware of my own nakedness in a way that was new to me, wild and fresh and animalistic. In this house were seven alpha males —and I was supposed to mate with them all, join my bodies to theirs.

Two down … and five to go.

My cheeks flamed red as I hit the staircase and darted up it, grabbing a bloodred robe with a black silk interior and throwing it over my shoulders. To belt it closed would somehow feel like admitting that my sensuality, my sexuality, my nakedness was shameful to me, and I wouldn't do that. I wasn't some prudish human, crying foul at the sight of a woman's nipple. How disgusting to treat one's body like that, to treat such natural acts as sinful.

I wouldn't do it.

But I was still an eighteen year old girl who'd not only lost her virginity in the last few days but also screwed some random guy she'd just met. I was reeling a little bit.

"I can't remember," Tidus Hahn was saying as I came back down the stairs, "do we have to wear our alpha silver to this thing?"

"Does it sound like an uncomfortable hell to do so?" Che returned, standing naked and half-aroused next to the couch. I tried my best not to look down, but it was difficult—there were penises *everywhere*. "Then yeah, we probably have to wear that crap."

"Mostly I just feel sorry for Zara," Tidus said, turning to glance over his shoulder at me. His smile was bright, like the sun on the sea, and his skin was the sweet bronze of summer days and salty waves. His eyes, they were a soft dove gray, and his hair … it was a dirty blonde that gave him this charming, surfer sort of a look. Even though we'd just met, I liked him. "I mean, if one piece of silver makes me want to cut my own arm off, what's it like to wear *eight*?"

"Don't worry about me," I told him as I avoided looking at Che. "I'm the Alpha Female; I can handle it."

Tidus rolled his ashy gray eyes at me, but he never stopped smiling.

"Oh come on, you might be Alpha, but you're still human."

"I am werewolf," I said, but he just laughed.

"Yeah, werewolf. Half-human, half-wolf."

"No," I corrected as I paused between him and Che, "all werewolf. We're a completely different species."

"Maybe," the Alpha-Son of Pack of Amber Ash said as he grinned at me, "but you can't deny that there's still some humanity in there." He reached out and poked me in the bare chest with a finger. "It's okay to hurt a little; it's okay to admit that we're all fallible."

His words were a mimicry of what Montgomery had already told me—that I didn't have to do this alone, that I didn't have to be perfect. So why did it feel like I was already failing miserably?

Nic was upset; I was confused; my mother was pissed; the vampires and witches were ganging up on us, kidnapping us, draining us dry and eating our flesh. I refused to ask myself if things could get any worse because I knew that the second I did … they probably would.

Instead, I just smiled back at Tidus.

"Maybe," is the only response I could come up with. I was used to being in charge, used to making things happen, used to knowing what to do and how to do it. This, this floundering and this uncertainty was all new to me.

"Is your boyfriend done with the shower yet?" Silas Vetter asked, tracing a mindless finger over his scar. I turned my attention to my mate from Pack Obsidian Gold and found his amber eyes watching me carefully. If he was upset about what had happened between Che and me, he didn't let on. None of them did. "Because if he's going to keep on throwing a fucking fit, he may as well do it somewhere else."

"I'll check on him," I said, my gaze panning over Jax, Anubis, and Montgomery. They were all sitting in the living room, various expressions of confusion, exhaustion, and worry scrawled across their handsome features. As if they could sense me staring, they all glanced up in almost perfect unison. "We should probably hurry and get out to the banquet," I said absently, more to myself than to them.

I had enough to worry about without pissing my mother off even more than I already had.

Nic was sitting on the floor of the tiled shower when I let myself into the bathroom. There was no lock on the door— the Pairing House was designed to accommodate the closeness of an alpha pair after all—or else I'd have probably had to break the damn thing down.

She huffed and she puffed and she blew the house down ... But even nursery rhyme jokes weren't enough to make me chuckle, not with the dejected look on my bodyguard-turned-mate's face.

"I knew it had to happen eventually," he whispered after I'd dropped my robe and stepped into the tiled space beside him. Folding my legs, I sat down opposite Nic and let the warm water, fresh soapy smell, and the woodsy scent of another Ebon Red pack member surround me. "I just didn't expect it to happen so soon," he added when I didn't respond.

"I didn't plan it," I told him, not sure why I even felt the need to defend myself. Nic was lucky to be a part of the Pairing at all and here he was complaining about my mating with another male? But at the same time, I understood. I understood and I felt like shit about it. "Although Nikolina did order me to ..."

"That's not why you did it," he told me because he knew me just as well as I knew myself. Maybe better. Yeah, probably better. "You're attracted to him."

"I am," I said, because I couldn't and wouldn't deny it. And there was no way in hell I was lying to Nic, not now, not when I needed him by my side more than ever before. If we were going to survive this thing and come out victorious on the other side—and that was a big if—then we needed to be a team. No, more than just a team; we needed to be a *pack*. Werewolves versus vampires had sketchy enough odds. Werewolves versus vampires *and* witches was an impossibility. Werewolves and faeries versus a kingdom and a coven … that would take some political maneuvering I wasn't sure I was capable of.

Silence fell between us as hot water pounded our matching red hair, our backs, the tiles on the floor around us.

"I'm sorry," I told Nic, reaching out and putting a hand on his knee. He flinched a little at the touch, licked his lips and glanced away. "Not for mating with Che, but for the way I did it. I should've waited, talked to you first. You're more than just another alpha male in the pairing, Nic. You're … my right hand."

"Maybe your left?" he asked with a slight smile, and I knew he was joking about his usual position, standing behind and to the left of me. It was where an alpha's bodyguard always stood.

"Okay, my left," I said with a matching smile. Nic glanced up at me and the expression faded a little. He was jealous; that was okay. I expected him to be jealous. It was only natural.

He blinked wet lashes over dark eyes and then sighed.

"The last thing I want to do is cause you more trouble, Zara. You've got enough on your plate as it is. I just …" Nic closed his eyes for a moment and took a deep breath. "I just wish you were mine."

"I am," I said, getting onto my knees and crawling closer to him, so I could brush some dark red hair from his face. He opened his crow black eyes to stare into mine, telling me without words that he loved me, that he'd do anything for me, that we'd fight through this together. The one thing neither of us mentioned was that at the end of the Pairing, I'd be expected to choose one mate. Just one. And we both knew the other packs would never accept both an Ebon Red Alpha Female *and* an Ebon Red Alpha Male.

That was a problem for another day.

"Do you forgive me?" I asked as I dropped a thumb to the moist curve of Nic's lower lip.

"There's nothing to forgive you for," he said, but I shook my head, wet hair clinging to the sides of my face.

My mother might say a leader never acknowledged their own mistakes, but … what kind of leader—what kind of *mate*—would I be to these men if I didn't at least take their feelings into consideration? It was hard enough for Nic to see me dating other guys. I could've given him a heads-up about the sex, talked to him about it first, let him know my intentions. Maybe I didn't *have* to, but I could have. In the future, I'd remember that.

"Next time, I'll warn you first."

Nic's mouth twitched, somewhere between a smile and a frown.

"So … before you sleep with yet another guy, you'll ask my permission?"

My turn to smile.

"No. But I'll admit to my own intentions."

Nic sighed again and bit his lip for a moment.

"Okay," he said, with another of those half-smile, half-frown things, "I forgive you and I accept. But I don't like it."

"I know," I said, leaning in through the hot steam to press a smoldering kiss to his wet lips.

Nic might not like it, but this was our future.

For the next year, the seven of us would live together, work together, sleep together.

And hopefully … ensure that our people actually had a future to look forward to.

So. The fate of the werewolves, an ancient people born from mother earth's womb, rested on the shoulders of a bunch of hormone crazy young adults.

How scary is that?

Monday morning rolled around and with it, a whole storm cloud of issues followed. On the one hand, I was glad that the Pairing Ceremony was officially over. It was something I'd been dreading for months and now, it was done. Not only that, but I still had Nic with me, standing by my side in the parking lot outside the Triad Historical Society.

On my right, I had Che, the connection between us throbbing and pulsing like a live thing. I knew Nic could tell, but he did a damn good job pretending he didn't notice. At the very least, it felt like Che was trying *not* to rub it in his face today. Smart choice on his part.

"Let's get in and get out," I said, the rest of my boys fanned out behind me. Montgomery held up the rear, his arsenal of weapons enhanced with a few extra bone knives. I was also rocking my badass tool kit, just in case.

"That's what *she* said," Tidus whispered under his breath, and then chuckled, his mood as lighthearted as always. I gave him a quick look over my shoulder and a small half-smile that didn't quite reach my eyes.

I *had* included protection for the pack until the night

after we picked up the map from the witches. But I'd also fucked them pretty hard with my end of the bargain. Suffice it to say, they were *not* going to be happy to see me here. I needed to keep my guard up.

'Keep your eyes on the cats,' I added in wolfspeak, leading the alpha males through the wrought iron gate and onto the property. Up ahead, a gray and white cat crouched, opening its mouth in a violent pink tongued hiss. It swiped at us and then disappeared into the bushes.

'Back in the day,' Anubis said as I ascended the steps and made my way to the front door, *'when my alpha-father was in charge of the pack, he bought more than just witch hazel from the local coven.'*

I paused at the door and lifted my nose to the air, trying to sniff out either the metallic-floral scent of magic or the stink of witches. I got nothing. Either there weren't any spells waiting in hiding for us out here, or else Coven Triad had just done an incredible job covering it all up.

'Crimson Dusk had anti-magic charms to wear around their necks. They activated whenever a spell was cast on them.' Anubis paused his story as I lifted my hand to knock. No way was I walking straight in there, not this time. Although the sign on the front *did* say *Open* … Technically a curious human could waltz in here at any moment for a tour.

Goddess help them if they did.

"What's your point?" Silas asked aloud, lighting a cigarette and eyeing the old Victorian house with distaste. It was a beautiful building, at least aesthetically speaking, but

I could understand the twisted scowl on his lips.

Even if it didn't reek of magic, even if there were no outward signs of malice, there was just this feeling in the air that no amount of witch hazel could ever hide. As I stood there, I couldn't help but wonder—were the missing pack members below my feet? Trapped in the witches' catacombs beneath the building? And if they were, how the hell was I going to get them out?

"I'm just saying," Anubis said aloud, sounding slightly irritated. "That they'd be nice to have right now. I feel like I'm about two seconds from being blown up."

I knocked again, glancing over as Che sneaked along the deck, cupping his hands and trying to peer through the glass and the gauzy curtains inside.

"Zara," Montgomery growled, his voice low and menacing.

I turned around to find the Maiden standing at the end of the walkway, her pointed witch hat tilted to one side, her lips painted a bright purple and dotted with silver sparkles. Even from here, I could see the bits of iron and silver pierced through her lips, her nose, her ears. And there was no missing the tattoo that wound around her wrist, the one that sealed her into the bargain with me.

"Don't trust what you see through that glass," she said, her voice a low, even keel that gave nothing away. "The windows are spelled to keep everything looking peaceful and serene. It could be a bloodbath in there and you'd never know."

I exchanged a glance with Nic and headed down the

stairs, a knot of wolves around me, all of them in human form, all of them dressed casually enough to be seen in public. It felt good to be surrounded like that, in the center of a whole mess of backup.

"Glamour?" I asked as I moved forward and took the point of the group again. Nic followed along, sticking to my left side as usual. And Che? He was on my right, as if *he* were a guard, too. When I looked over at him, he blinked at me and cocked a brow like he didn't know why I was staring. I refused to admit that I found his lazy bad boy slouch attractive.

Just yesterday, we'd had *sex* for the first time ever, our bodies joined in primal heat. If I looked at Che for too long, I could still feel the wild thrust of his hips, his warm breath feathering against my neck …

Deep breath and focus, *Zara Wolf. Deal with the witches first and then boy troubles later.*

"You could call it that," the witch said, reaching up to adjust her hat. Her brown-blonde curls cascaded out the bottom, twisted with bits of ribbon, beads, even bones. None of it was there for aesthetic purposes. No, each one of those items was a *weapon*.

"You have our map?" I asked, cutting to the chase and crossing my arms over my chest. I needed to get this damn thing and get the hell out of here before the coven decided how, exactly, they wanted to pay me back for the stunt I'd pulled the other day.

To be fair, they *were* rounding up my people and *eating* them; it was hard to imagine they could do much worse.

17

My skin rippled with disgust, and it took every ounce of self-control I had to fight back my anger. The missing pack members could be *right* here on this property, and I wouldn't know it, had no way to get to them. Penetrating the bubble of power around this place, it wasn't happening without a whole lot more help and a whole fuck of a lot of casualties.

Nikolina would be willing to pay the price; I was not.

"There are two maps in my pocket," the girl said, dressed in a black leather half-jacket, a purple crop top, and skinny jeans with heels. If it weren't for the hat and the piercings, I'd almost believe she was your average, everyday college student. Even the items stuck all over her jacket could be written off by the average person. *I* knew they were all spells, but most humans wouldn't think twice about a tiny bird skull pendant on a girl's jacket—especially not in Eugene, Oregon. "One of them is the real map and the other, a manipulation of the magic that the Crone wants me to give you."

Both my brows went up.

"Excuse me?"

"Look," the girl said, and I sensed a ripple of magic around us, something small, barely noticeable but definitely *there*. Another glamour? "Not everyone trapped in this nightmare *likes* the way things are going, you see where I'm coming from?"

"Not particularly," I said as Nic scoffed from beside me and Jax let out a low growl.

"I'm going to give you both maps: only one of them is real," she continued, ignoring my comment as she pulled a